THE WORLD OF MARTIAL ARTS

MARTIAL ARTS MOVIES

BY JIM OLLHOFF

Visit us at
www.abdopublishing.com

Published by ABDO Publishing Company, 8000 West 78th Street, Suite 310, Edina, MN 55439.
Copyright ©2008 by Abdo Consulting Group, Inc. International copyrights reserved in all countries.
No part of this book may be reproduced in any form without written permission from the publisher.
ABDO & Daughters™ is a trademark and logo of ABDO Publishing Company.

Printed in the United States.

Editor: John Hamilton
Graphic Design: Sue Hamilton
Cover Design: Neil Klinepier
Cover Illustration: Getty Images
Interior Photos and Illustrations: p 1 Jackie Chan, AP Images; p 3 Ranger Bob in *Proboscis,* courtesy
Sparrow Media Group; p 5 Bruce Lee in *Enter the Dragon,* AP Images; p 7 Bruce Lee in *The Green Hornet,*
AP Images; p 8 (top) United States movie poster for *Enter the Dragon,* courtesy Warner Bros. Pictures;
(bottom) Chinese movie poster for *Enter the Dragon,* courtesy Golden Harvest Entertainment Co.;
p 9 Bruce Lee, Getty Images; p 11 Chuck Norris, AP Images; p 12 *Snake in the Eagle's Shadow,* courtesy
Sony Pictures; p 13 Jackie Chan, Getty Images; p 14 Jackie Chan in a silly pose, AP Images; p 15 Jackie
Chan in *Rush Hour,* Corbis; p 17 Cynthia Rothrock, Corbis; p 18 Michelle Yeoh in *Crouching Tiger,
Hidden Dragon,* Corbis; p 19 David Carradine, Getty Images; p 20 Jean-Claude Van Damme, Corbis;
p 21 (top) Tony Jaa, AP Images; (bottom) Brandon Lee, Corbis; p 22 Jet Li, Corbis; p 23 (top) Steven
Segal, Getty Images; (bottom) Sammo Hung, Getty Images; p 25 Bruce Lee in *The Chinese Connection,*
Corbis; p 26 *Mr. Vampire* character, courtesy Star TV Filmed Entertainment; p 27 Stephen Chow, Getty
Images; p 28 Akira Kurosawa's *Seven Samurai,* courtesy Toho Company, p 29 scene from *Crouching Tiger,
Hidden Dragon,* Getty Images; p 31 Chuck Norris and Bruce Lee in *The Way of the Dragon,* Getty Images.

Library of Congress Cataloging-in-Publication Data

Ollhoff, Jim, 1959-
  Martial arts movies / Jim Ollhoff.
      p. cm. -- (The world of martial arts)
  Includes index.
  ISBN 978-1-59928-980-9
  1. Martial arts films--History and criticism. I. Title.

PN1995.9.H3O45 2008
791.43'655--dc22

                              2007030550

武道

CONTENTS

Right: Ranger Bob Trooper takes a kick in the 2000 film *Proboscis.* Some martial arts movies are good, some not so good, but all are fun to watch.

INTRODUCTION

"Your kung fu is no good! I will teach you a lesson!" And so begins a 10-minute movie fight scene. The combatants fight in jerky, tightly choreographed punches and kicks. They fly through the air, leap to the top of buildings, and do somersaults before delivering punches. In the end, of course, the hero wins. The villain learns an important lesson about goodness, friendship, or integrity.

A martial arts movie is simply an action film with a lot of martial arts fighting. The category began soon after film was invented, with most of the movies coming out of China and Hong Kong. The number of movies swelled in the 1970s, with hundreds of films pouring out of Asia. Some of the movies were good, some not so good, but all were fun to watch.

Most of the Asian movies that came to the United States from the 1970s to the 1990s were made by a Hong Kong company called Golden Harvest. (At that time, Hong Kong was a colony of Great Britain. Today it is a part of China.) Golden Harvest produced many of the movies, which means it paid to make them. Golden Harvest was also a distributor. The company duplicated film footage and made copies available to theaters in the United States. Most of the films of Bruce Lee, Jackie Chan, and Jet Li were produced and distributed by Golden Harvest. It was not the first company to enter the film markets of Western countries, but it was the first to have staying power.

Today, producers from all over the world make martial arts movies. The United States is one of the chief producers of martial arts films.

Above: Bruce Lee signed on with production company Golden Harvest in 1971. He starred in six martial arts movies with this Hong Kong production company. Several became very popular, including *Enter the Dragon*, his final picture.

BRUCE LEE

Bruce Lee was one of the most famous martial artists of all time. Through his movies, he made martial arts well known in the United States. His careful technique, his extreme speed, and his charming acting ability made him popular. His movies also made many people in the United States want to study the martial arts.

Bruce Lee was born on November 27, 1940. Chinese calendars call years by animal names. Lee was born in the Year of the Dragon. His mother and father, both Chinese, had been traveling in the United States. Lee was born in San Francisco, California. When he was three months old, his parents returned with him to Hong Kong.

He grew up in Hong Kong excelling at dancing, physical fitness, and of course, martial arts. His father was an actor, and Bruce loved movies and acting. By the time he was 18 years old, he had already appeared in 20 films.

Bruce Lee moved to the United States in 1959, and got a job as a dancing instructor. He enrolled at the University of Washington, studying philosophy and teaching kung fu. In 1964, he participated in a karate tournament. There, a Hollywood insider noticed Lee. Before long, he was auditioning for parts in Hollywood. He landed a role in the TV series *The Green Hornet* (1966-1967). Even though the series only lasted for one season, Lee made a lasting impression on movie producers.

Facing page: In the 1966-1967 TV series *The Green Hornet*, Bruce Lee played Kato, an Asian valet and martial arts expert.

During this time, Bruce Lee explored his understanding of martial arts. The style he had learned in Hong Kong was *wing chun* kung fu. Lee began developing his own martial art style. He would later call his style *jeet kun do*. He wrote a number of books on his philosophy of the martial arts, as well as the techniques of jeet kun do.

Lee began working on story ideas with Hollywood producers. He had an idea about a television series featuring a Chinese monk in the American Wild West. The studio welcomed the idea, and Lee hoped to play the role. However, in the end, the studio gave the role to actor David Carradine. The popular series was *Kung Fu*, which aired from 1972 to 1975.

Below: The English and Chinese movie posters for Bruce Lee's classic film *Enter The Dragon.*

After a few more tries to start his movie career, Lee went back to Hong Kong. He worked with the Golden Harvest movie studio to produce a 1971 movie called *Fists of Fury*. It broke box office records in Hong Kong. Later that year, he starred in another Hong Kong hit movie called *The Chinese Connection.* For his next movie, *Return of the Dragon* (1972), Lee not only starred, but also directed.

In 1972, Lee started a film called *Game of Death*. However, he put the movie on hold when he secured a deal with an American film company, Warner Brothers. In the first cooperative film effort between an American film company and a Hong Kong film company, Lee made *Enter the Dragon* (1973). Lee played a martial artist invited to a secret tournament on an island. Lee's character had to go undercover to find evidence to convict the tournament organizer of various crimes. Many people consider *Enter the Dragon* to be the most important martial arts movie ever made. Lee finished making the movie, but tragically, never saw the premiere.

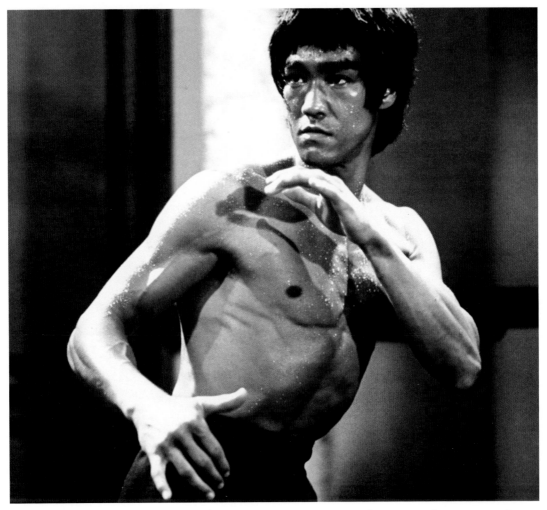

Lee developed a headache on July 20, 1973. He took a prescription medicine, and then went to sleep. He lapsed into a coma, and died soon afterwards. The cause of death was a cerebral edema, a buildup of fluid in the brain. Doctors said that Lee had a severe allergic reaction to the headache medication, which caused the edema.

The world lost a great actor, teacher, and author on that day. His dedication to the martial arts and his other goals have inspired untold numbers of people. Almost single-handedly, he changed the world of martial arts.

Above: Bruce Lee takes a fighting stance. His untimely death at the age of 32 was a severe blow to martial arts movie fans around the world.

Chuck Norris

Chuck Norris was born on March 10, 1940, in Oklahoma. He joined the Air Force after high school, and was stationed in South Korea. It was there he began to learn martial arts, studying the art of *tang soo do*. He pursued the martial arts, and eventually began to fight in tournaments, which led to a number of national championships.

Norris got into the movie business by starring in *Return of the Dragon* with Bruce Lee. He played a bad guy who fights with Lee at the end of the film. His later films include *Good Guys Wear Black* (1977), *A Force of One* (1978), and *The Octagon* (1979). In 1982, he played a Texas Ranger in the movie *Lone Wolf McQuade*. He later portrayed a Texas Ranger again for the TV series *Walker, Texas Ranger*. Norris is most famous for this series, which aired from 1993 to 2001. Norris has been in more than 30 movies. He likes to play tough characters who have a clear knowledge of right from wrong.

Norris is active in a variety of humanitarian causes. He is a spokesperson for United Way and the Veterans Administration. He has been active in the Make A Wish Foundation, an organization that grants wishes to terminally ill children. In 1990, Norris was instrumental in starting the organization now known as Kick Start. This is a successful program to teach martial arts to high-risk kids.

Facing page: Martial arts champion Chuck Norris played many tough-guy roles in movies and TV shows, using his skills to subdue wrongdoers.

JACKIE CHAN

Perhaps the most famous martial artist in the world today is Jackie Chan. He has starred in more than 60 movies. His comedy, slapstick, and excellent martial arts skills have made him one of the biggest action stars in the world.

Jackie Chan was born in Hong Kong on April 7, 1954. His parents had steady jobs, but they were very poor. Every morning before work, Chan and his father practiced kung fu together. His father believed that kung fu helped build courage and character in his young son.

When Chan was seven years old, his parents enrolled him at the China Drama Academy (also called the Peking Opera School). He learned martial arts, acting, acrobatics, and singing. He spent the next 10 years of his life there, learning the skills he still uses today in his films.

In the 1970s, the Hong Kong film industry grew rapidly. Many martial arts films were produced, and they needed stuntmen. Stuntmen did the dangerous work—falling, taking hits, and other acrobatics. Chan was very athletic, and became a good stuntman. Chan developed a reputation for being willing to do almost any kind of dangerous stunt. Soon he was in great demand. He was a stuntman in two of Bruce Lee's films, *Fists of Fury* and *Enter the Dragon*.

Chan brought humor to his movies. His first big successes were *Snake in the Eagle's Shadow* and *Drunken Master* in 1978. In 1979, he directed and starred in *Fearless Hyena*, which was also a big hit.

Below: Jackie Chan's first big success was *Snake in the Eagle's Shadow.*

Above: Jackie Chan's humor and martial arts skills have made him famous.

Jackie Chan became a huge success in Asia. However, he wanted to also star in American movies. He got the opportunity to do a few Hollywood movies, including *The Big Brawl* (1980) and *Cannonball Run* (1984). Both were delightful films, but bad marketing and Chan's poor English language skills hindered his success. Finally, in 1994, he starred in *Rumble in the Bronx.* Even though it was filmed in Canada, this movie made Jackie Chan a hit with American audiences. Chan followed these movies with *Rush Hour* (1999) and *Shanghai Noon* (2000), which were huge hits in the United States.

People around the world know Jackie Chan for his comic timing and his creative fight scenes. He can take almost any object and turn it into a weapon. He fought people using sawhorses in *The Big Brawl*, grocery carts in *Rumble in the Bronx,* and animal skulls in *Shanghai Noon.* He became famous for doing all his own outrageous stunts, some of which were quite dangerous.

Chan continues making films, although he often prefers Hong Kong productions, where he has greater creative input. Chan also is an ambassador for the United Nation's Children's Fund (UNICEF), which takes up much of his time.

Left: Known for his physical humor, Jackie Chan strikes a silly pose.

Above: Famous for his outrageous stunts, Jackie Chan prepares to defend himself using a pool cue in the successful 1999 movie *Rush Hour.* Chan carefully choreographs fight scenes, using almost any object as a weapon. Since Chan does all his own stunts, the actor has injured himself with sprains, broken bones, and even concussions. When asked how many bones he's broken, Chan responded in an E! Celebrity online question-and-answer forum, "I cannot remember—a lot! My arms, shoulders, ribs. Crack, crack, crack. Broken, broken, broken."

Cynthia Rothrock

Often called "the queen of martial arts movies," Cynthia Rothrock starred in almost 50 films. She was born in Scranton, Pennsylvania, on March 8, 1957. She began taking martial arts lessons when she was 13. In the 1980s, she hit the tournament circuit, winning many championships in both form and weapons competitions. Soon, Hong Kong producers invited her to Asia to star in movies.

Her first martial arts movie was *Yes Madam* (1985), directed by Corey Yuen, a good friend of Jackie Chan. This movie was not only the start of Rothrock's career, but also of the famous Malaysian actress Michelle Yeoh.

Rothrock's many successful films include *China O'Brien* (1990), *Lady Dragon* (1992), and *Tiger Claws* (1992). She has worked with some of the biggest names in the martial arts world. She helped to pioneer women's roles in action films.

Rothrock has studied many martial arts styles. She holds black belts in tang soo do, tae kwon do, eagle claw kung fu, and northern Shaolin kung fu.

Black Belt magazine once compared Rothrock to her male movie star counterparts, saying she "obliterates bad guys, but does it while perched on three-inch heels."

Above: Cynthia Rothrock has starred in nearly 50 martial arts films. She is known as "the queen of martial arts movies."

OTHER MOVIE MARTIAL ARTISTS

Below: Michelle Yeoh starred as martial artist Yu Shu Lien in the Oscar-winning film *Crouching Tiger, Hidden Dragon.*

Michelle Yeoh is an exciting performer. She starred in several martial arts films, even though she has had little martial arts training. Born in Malaysia on August 6, 1962, most of her films have been produced in Hong Kong. Her martial arts films include *Police Story 3: Supercop* (1992), *The Heroic Trio* (1993), *Tai Chi Master* (1993), and *Wing Chun* (1994). She also starred in *Crouching Tiger, Hidden Dragon* (2000).

Left: David Carradine became famous as the martial arts star of the TV series *Kung Fu,* which ran from 1972 to 1975.

David Carradine was born on December 8, 1936. He was the son of actor John Carradine, who was famous for his creepy roles in horror movies. David Carradine has starred in more than 20 movies, but is most famous for his portrayal of the gentle Kwai Chang Caine in the TV series *Kung Fu* (1972 to 1975). Carradine played a half-Chinese Buddhist monk, searching for his brother in the American Wild West. He helped to popularize the martial arts with his role in the series.

One of the martial arts movie heroes of the 1990s was Jean-Claude Van Damme. He was born October 18, 1960, in Belgium. He began to study *shotokan* karate at age 10. He also took up ballet and weightlifting. His muscular physique earned him the nickname "the muscles from Brussels." His breakout role was *Bloodsport* (1988), about a mixed martial arts tournament. His filmography includes more than 30 movies. His most successful films were produced in the late 1980s and early 1990s. These included *Kickboxer* (1989), *Universal Soldier* (1992), *Hard Target* (1993), *Street Fighter* (1994), and *Sudden Death* (1995). His most acclaimed movie is *Timecop* (1994), in which he plays a police officer from the future, after the invention of time machines. His character patrols time, making sure people do not use time machines to change history.

Left: Jean-Claude Van Damme was nicknamed "the muscles from Brussels." He combined weightlifting with the sport of karate. Two of his most popular films were *Universal Soldier* and *Timecop*.

A rising martial arts star today is Tony Jaa, from Thailand. He was born February 5, 1976. He grew up watching the movies of Bruce Lee, Jackie Chan, and Jet Li, and wanted to be in the movies. Beginning as a stuntman, his breakout role was as the star of *Ong-Bak* (2005). In this film, Jaa must retrieve a sacred object that bandits have stolen from a tiny village in Thailand. Jaa is an expert in *muay Thai*, a martial art that emphasizes the use of elbows and knees, along with fists and feet.

Brandon Lee, the son of Bruce Lee, was born February 1, 1965, in Oakland, California. He studied acting in college and learned martial arts from his father's top student, Danny Inosanto. Brandon had much of the speed, athleticism, and creativity of his father, as demonstrated by his movies *Laser Mission* (1990), *Showdown in Little Tokyo* (1991), and *Rapid Fire* (1992). His breakout role would have been the 1994 movie *The Crow.* Tragically, an accident cut short his promising career. While filming the last few scenes of the movie, a gun misfired and shot Brandon. He died at the hospital. With the support of Brandon's mother and fiancé, the director completed the movie using stunt doubles and special effects.

Tony Jaa

Brandon Lee

Above: Champion martial artist Jet Li began acting at the age of 19 and continues to star in movies today.

Another remarkable martial arts actor is Jet Li, who was born in China on April 26, 1963. By the late 1970s, Li had become a Chinese champion of martial arts. In the early 1980s, he took up acting. He starred in more than 20 movies in China, including the popular *Once Upon a Time in China* (1991), in which he portrayed the Chinese folk hero Wong Fei Hung. Li made the jump to Hollywood movies in 1998. His first United States picture was *Lethal Weapon 4* (1998). He also started the Jet Li One Foundation Project, dedicated to helping adolescents in China who suffer from mental illness.

Steven Segal hit the martial arts film scene with a 1988 action movie called *Above the Law*. He played a tough cop who unravels an international mystery. It opened to good reviews. In 1992, Segal made *Under Siege*, in which he played a cook on an aircraft carrier that was taken over by terrorists.

Segal has made many other movies since then, but most have bypassed the theaters and gone straight to video and DVD. Steven Segal's career is unusual because his fighting style is *aikido*, which emphasizes grabbing and grappling instead of kicks and punches.

Above: Steven Segal in *Fire Down Below*.

Sammo Hung is not well known in the United States. However, he is a major force in Asian martial arts cinema. Born in Hong Kong on January 7, 1952, Hung was a classmate of Jackie Chan in the China Drama Academy. They became good friends, and have been cooperating on movies ever since. Hung directed, produced, starred, or choreographed the fighting for more than 150 films. He enjoys making comedy martial arts movies. He has surprisingly acrobatic abilities despite being a man of large frame.

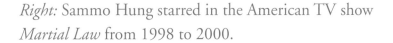

Right: Sammo Hung starred in the American TV show *Martial Law* from 1998 to 2000.

How to Watch Kung Fu Cinema

Many early kung fu movies were filmed on very low budgets. Therefore, they didn't have a lot of money for fancy sets or special effects. That's why much of the fighting happens in forests or on very bare movie sets. Watch for signs of low budgets and ways the producers tried to cut costs.

When watching with the subtitles on, enjoy the English words. They are often translated by people who don't know English very well. This frequently leads to comical dialogue. If you listen to the English dubs, enjoy the voices. The English voice actors try to match the mouth movements of the Chinese-speaking actors. The results are sometimes hilarious. It's always fun to hear the voices of the characters, listening for whoever has the whiney voice, and who has the gruff, tough voice.

Many martial arts movies center on a hero who is very advanced at the martial arts. The hero can defeat large groups of enemies just because he or she is so talented and skilled. The evil character in the movies tends to also be very good in the martial arts, leading to an inevitable showdown.

Above: Bruce Lee stars as Chen Zhen, a martial artist investigating the mystery of his teacher's death, in *The Chinese Connection.*

Many Chinese kung fu movies play on the fact that there are many different styles of kung fu. The movies will be about one school competing against another school. Is wing chun kung fu better than the fighting sticks kung fu? Is iron hand kung fu better than jumping dragon kung fu? Many Chinese kung fu movies use these kinds of questions as a plot. When students of one style come up against students of another style, they are bound to say, "Your style is no good!"

Another common element in Chinese kung fu movies is "the special technique." This is an imaginary kick, strike, or series of movements that will defeat any attacker. In some movies, people search for a secret scroll or book that reveals the special technique. In other movies, a student will beg to learn the secret technique from an old, wise master. If a stranger comes along and learns the secret technique, he or she instantly becomes invincible. In the 2005 comedy *Kung Fu Hustle*, a con man sold a book of secret martial arts techniques.

Revenge becomes a common motivator in many martial arts movies. Most commonly, someone from one school kills the master teacher of another school. Then, the grieving students go out for revenge. A famous line heard in these movies is, "You killed my master!" Bruce Lee's character in *The Chinese Connection* grieves over the suspicious death of his teacher, and then takes action.

Some movies make use of real cultural myths that might be unfamiliar to most Americans. In Chinese mythology, people used to believe in the *jiangshi*, a vampire-like creature. The jiangshi were people who had died, but didn't get a proper burial in their hometown.

Below: A hopping vampire from the 1985 movie *Mr. Vampire.*

Above: Director and star Stephen Chow stands next to a poster for his humorous film *Kung Fu Hustle.* Chow also co-wrote the movie, which was inspired by martial arts films that he enjoyed. Set in 1930s Shanghai, China, the movie features Sing (Chow), a boy who wants to do good, but fails. Sing decides that bad guys always win, and sets out to join a gang. However, people and events change his mind.

The jiangshi wanted to get back to their hometown, but because they were dead, they couldn't move their legs. Therefore, they had to hop back to their hometown to get a proper burial. The hilarious movie *Mr. Vampire* (1985) features many of these dreaded hopping vampires.

Some martial arts movies weave facts and myths. The delightful 1993 film *Iron Monkey* portrays another common myth—a man who steals from the rich and corrupt, and gives to the poor. It also portrays the Chinese folk hero Wong Fei Hung as a child.

Some movies use real kung fu styles but add a new twist. There is a fighting technique called drunken kung fu. It is very deceptive in its lunges, sways, and steps. The technique makes the person look like he's drunk. In 1994's *The Legend of Drunken Master* (also called *Drunken Master II*), Jackie Chan plays a martial artist who battles an evil gang. He accidentally drinks liquor, which allows him to fight drunken style kung fu, making him nearly invincible. Many people believe the movie's final fight scene is one of the finest ever filmed.

Some martial arts movies are true epics. *Seven Samurai* (1954), by Japanese director Akira Kurosawa, is a movie about a town under siege by bandits. The villagers hire seven Japanese samurai to protect them. It's a movie about honor and courage, and has inspired many movies since then. The American Western *The Magnificent Seven* (1960) is one of many movies inspired by *Seven Samurai*.

In many martial arts movies, characters do fantastic things. They fly through the air to perform kicks, they do multiple somersaults, and they jump great distances. To perform these amazing stunts, the actors are often suspended in the air by wires. Sometimes, Americans call this kind of filmmaking "wire fu."

Below: The 1954 Academy Award-nominated *Seven Samurai* became Japan's highest money-making film of its day. Directed by Akira Kurosawa, *Seven Samurai* is often listed as one of the best films of the 20th century.

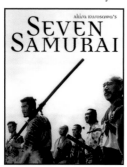

The movie *Crouching Tiger, Hidden Dragon* is an example of this. The characters leap into trees, run along the sides of walls, and leap long distances. This is part of the mythology of Asian martial arts, which says that if someone studies martial arts long enough, they can defy gravity and other laws of physics. It's similar to American Western movies, in which gunslingers shoot with uncanny accuracy. For example, they can shoot the gun out of the bad guy's hand from across the street. In real life, their guns were terribly inaccurate. Gunslingers had to shoot several times at people who were only a few yards away. Their guns produced so much smoke that they had to run around the clouds of smoke to find their opponent.

Martial arts movies are full of action, fun, and drama. They are an exciting category of action movies. They are also a fun way to enjoy the martial arts.

Above: A scene from *Crouching Tiger, Hidden Dragon*. In 2001, the film won four Academy Awards, including one for Best Foreign Language Film.

GLOSSARY

Belt

Most modern martial arts schools use a system of colored belts to rank their students based on their abilities and length of training. Each school decides the exact order of belts, but most are similar in ranking. A typical school might start beginner students at white belt. From there, the students progress to gold belt, then green, purple, blue, red, and brown. The highest belt is black. It usually takes from three to five years of intense training to achieve a black belt.

Filmography

A list of films created by one actor or director. Also, a list of films in one subject, such as martial arts.

Kung Fu

A Chinese martial art that had an early influence on the development of other martial arts worldwide, such as karate. The phrase kung fu means "achievement through great effort."

Monk

A person who lives in a religious community. Monks usually take certain vows, such as nonviolence or poverty, to help them focus less on the distractions of the outside world. Buddhist monks from China's Shaolin Temple were some of the first to use kung fu, both as a method of exercise and self-defense, and as a way to clear the mind.

Muay Thai

A style of kickboxing that is very popular in the country of Thailand.

Philosophy

The study of knowledge and beliefs. A way of looking at the world and our place in it.

Samurai

The trained warrior class of medieval Japan.

Tae Kwon Do

A hard-style form of martial arts that originated from Korea. Tae kwon do is known for its powerful kicks. The phrase *tae kwon do* means "the way of kicking and punching."

Tournament

A series of contests, usually in a specific sport or game, between a number of competitors. Winners play winners, until only two people are left to compete. The winner of this final competition will be the ultimate champion.

Below: Chuck Norris fights Bruce Lee in *The Way of the Dragon.*

INDEX